This colouring book belongs to

....

For Poppy, I hope you ALWAYS love drawing and crafting. Keep following your dreams! Love, Auntie Em x

First published 2025 by Walker Books Ltd

87 Vauxhall Walk, London SE11 5HJ

10 9 8 7 6 5 4 3 2 1

EU Authorized Representative: HackettFlynn Ltd, 36 Cloch Choirneal, Balrothery, Co. Dublin, K32 C942, Ireland. EU@walkerpublishinggroup.com

This book has been typeset in Happynews

Printed in Scotland by Bell & Bain Ltd, Glasgow

British Library Cataloguing in Publication Data: a catalogue record for this book is available from the British Library

ISBN 978-1-5295-3312-5

www.walker.co.uk

FSC www.fsc.org MIX Paper | Supporting responsible forestry FSC® C007785

emily coxhead

colour your HAPPY

a cute and cosy colouring book

WALKER BOOKS
AND SUBSIDIARIES
LONDON • BOSTON • SYDNEY • AUCKLAND

COLOUR YOUR HAPPY

Hello! It's time for you to begin your cosy colouring adventure with me! Take a deep breath, follow the step-by-step instructions and get ready to colour yourself happy.

@thehappynewspaper @emilycoxhead

SHARE YOUR ART!

Don't forget to tag #ColourYourHappy to share your colourful creations with the world – let's see the magic you create!

LET'S GET STARTED

1. Pick your colours – the more colours the better!

2. Place a sheet of blank paper underneath the page you are colouring to stop the ink from bleeding through – that way your amazing art will stay neat and tidy.

3. Start colouring – use your imagination to bring your drawings to life!

TRY IT OUT HERE

KEEP
Smiling

Chill out

Bee
HAPPY

YAY

DEEP BREATHS

HAPPY THOUGHTS

yipee

YOU'RE
OUT
OF THIS
WORLD

SUNNY
DAYS

you're
llovely
hii

DREAM
BIG